MEGA MASH-UP

Pirates v Ancient Egyptians in a Haunted Museum

Draw your own adventure!

nosy crow

Mega Mash-Up: Pirates v Ancient Egyptians in a Haunted Museum

Published in the UK in 2011 by Nosy Crow Ltd

The Crow's Nest, 11 The Chandlery
50 Westminster Bridge Road
London, SE1 7QY, UK

ISBN: 978 085763 010 0

This book needs

YOU!

What if some bloodthirsty **Pirates**

and crazy **Ancient Egyptians**

broke into a HAUNTED MUSEUM?

Would one of them STEAL the

priceless Golden Howler Monkey?

Or would the Museum's SPOOKY

GHOSTS turn against them first?

You'll have to finish the illustrations
and find out...

Prepare to **LAUGH** while you doodle

and SNIGGER while you read.

Visit our awesome
website and get involved!
www.megamash-up.com
Upload artwork and get
the latest news

INTRODUCING the Pirates!

★ Bloodythirsty Jack ★

★ Scurvy Sid ★

★ Captain Curse ★

★ Beardy Belinda ★

★ Pete the Plank ★

INTRODUCING the Ancient Egyptians!

★ Niles ★

★ Pharo-Nuff ★

★ King Crypt ★

★ Marvin the Mummy ★

★ Bird-Head Horace ★

You'll need these...

DRAWING tools

These are the **3** tools that Nikalas and Tim have used to create the artwork in this book.

felt-tip pen or marker

pencil

wax crayon

Using different tools helps create great drawings

PEN

crayon

texture page

pen zigzags

crayon rubbing from lino floor

cross-hatching pencil

crayon rubbing from floor

pencil rubbing from wooden door

scribbly pencil

There are loads of ways you can add texture to your artwork. Here are a few examples

crayon rubbing from wall

pencil dashes

DRAWING TIP! Turn to the back of the book for ideas on stuff you might want to draw in this adventure

pen circles

Chapter 1

Monkey Business!

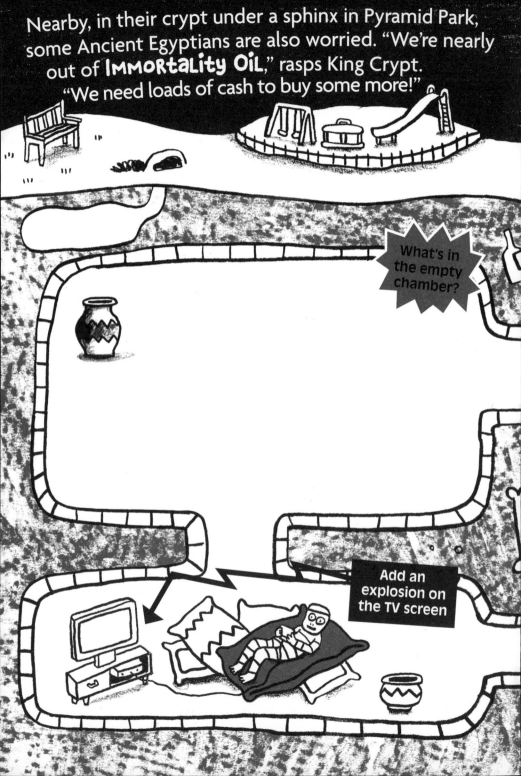

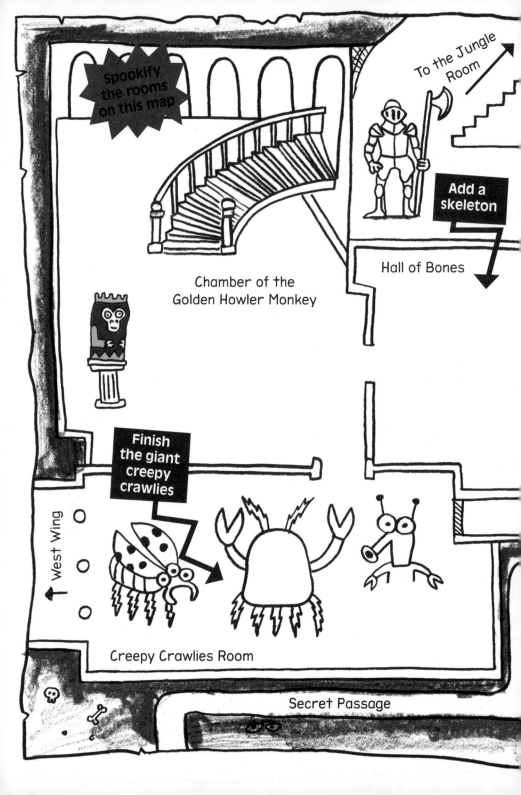

East Wing

Chamber of Horrors

Barmy Basement

The Pirates and the Ancient Egyptians both have a map of the town's **abandoned** Museum. Somewhere inside lies a priceless statue of a Golden Howler Monkey. Whoever steals it will be **MEGA-RICH**! But they must be quick - the museum is due to be demolished today!

"Come on, lads, let's go plunder the Museum!" cackles Captain Curse. "Got the cutlasses?" "CHECK!" hollers the crew. "**SPARE PANTS**?" "CHECKED!

Add some snacks

Add a digital camera

Add Captain Curse's hook

Who's taking the best stuff?

The Pirates pile on to the Number 42 bus. "Take us to the Museum as fast as ye can, Driver," growls Captain Curse. "Or we'll scuttle this bus!" "That'll be £2.80," replies the driver, **COOL AS CUSTARD**.

Who will get into the Museum first?
Who will find the priceless
Golden Howler Monkey? And who
will be scared witless by the
Museum's **SPOOKY** residents?

Add more bats to spooky up the sky!

That doesn't sound very friendly!

The Pirates decide to break into the Museum through the sewers.

"Arrr! This place be **STINKIER** than Scurvy Sid's socks!" cries Pete the Plank.

The Ancient Egyptians arrive at the Museum, too. "We'll sneak in through the basement," whispers King Crypt. "Ignore those signs – no one's going to knock down the Museum today!"

What do these signs say?

DUE FOR DEMOLITION TODAY

Egyp

Monsters

The Pirates pop up through the Museum's loos.
"We made it, **mateys**!" splutters Captain Curse,
waving a loo roll around victoriously.

"Now, let's go find us a Golden Howler Monkey!"

"Yikes!" shrieks Scurvy Sid. "**A MOULDY OLD MUMMY**!"
"We're black-hearted Pirates, 'ere to grab us the
Golden Howler Monkey!" spits Captain Curse.
"We're noble Ancient Egyptians," says King Crypt,
snootily. "And the Monkey will be yours over my
EMBALMED body!"

After **fighting** for five minutes, they make a pact. "Right, ye poxy old landlubbers," puffs Captain Curse. "You take that door and we'll take this 'un. Whosoever finds the Golden Howler Monkey first, keeps it."

Add an Oof! sound effect

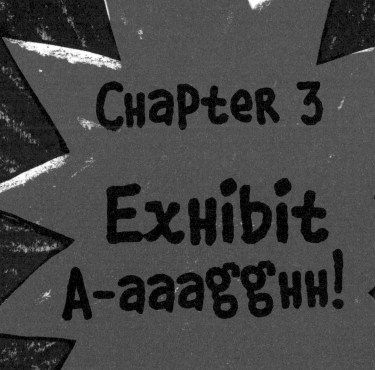

Chapter 3

Exhibit A-aaagghh!

The Pirates consult the map. "Oh no! We gotta go through the **CREEPY CRAWLIES** room," shudders Beardy Belinda. "And look — they're wriggling through the door!"

Make this door even more CREEPY!

Nervously, the Pirates go inside.
BUZZ! SWISH! SWOOOSH!
The creepy crawlies are **attacking**!

Meanwhile, the Ancient Egyptians have reached the Jungle Room. "What weird plants!" says Pharo-Nuff. "I must go closer... **AAAAGGGHHHH**!" Something has grabbed his ancient ankle. It's a monster vine!

What else is in the Jungle Room?

BaSh

Add more texture to the monster vine

Strange Sounds, suspiciously like singing, can be heard from below: "ALL RIGHT! EVERYBODY IN THE HOUSE SAY 'YEAH'!"

What sounds is the Golden Howler Monkey making?

CREAK, CRACK, CRASH! Pharo-Nuff has
CRASHED through a hole in the floor.
"I can see the **GOLDEN HOWLER MONKEY**!" yells
Pharo-Nuff. "And I can almost reach it!"

But the Pirates have reached the Chamber of the Golden Howler Monkey too. "I can hear singing behind that door!" cries Beardy Belinda, tapping her **HaiRy toe**.

The Pirates burst into the chamber, grabbing the Golden Howler Monkey from under Pharo-Nuff's noble nose.

Add some Ancient Egyptians peering through from upstairs

Finish the two-headed guard dog!

"MIND THE CROWN, MAN!" shrieks the statue in alarm. "Arrr, me beauty!" cackles Captain Curse. "You be comin' wiv us."

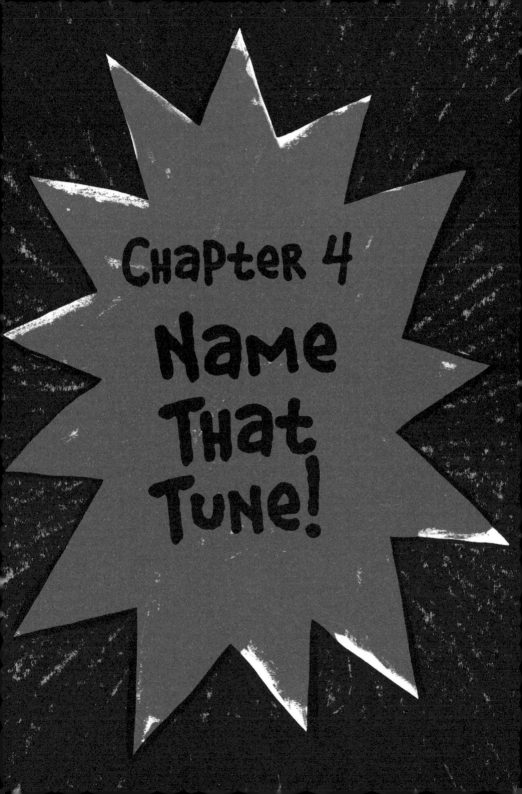

The stairs dump the Pirates back into the Chamber of the Golden Howler Monkey. "Serves you **SCaLLywaGS** right," laugh the Ancient Egyptians, snatching the priceless statue. "We're rich! RICH!"

YaY!

Add cheering sound effects

The Ancient Egyptians run into the next room with the Golden Howler Monkey. "Holy camel, it's **C-C-COLD** in here," complains Bird-Head Horace. "Must be the **Ice Age**!"

Draw a mammoth on the rampage

Exhausted and dizzy, the Pirates rush out of the Tunnel into a room full of shrunken heads. " 'Ave you seen any thievin' **OLD GEEZERS** wiv a Golden Howler Monkey?" Beardy Belinda asks one of them.

Add more heads on the plinths

He's a real nobody. Tee hee!

"Over there," it groans in reply. "Past the stuffed BEAR with one arm." In all the excitement, no one hears a **buLLDOZeR** starting its engine...

Scribble texture the bear

Who's grinning in the mirror?

"There's one of them!" gurgles Scurvy Sid, pointing at a disappearing Ancient Egyptian. "Aaargh! Look at that ARMCHAIR! It's got eyes and teeth. Grab an axe, we'll 'ave to hack our way through!"

The Pirates follow the Ancient Egyptians into the **HALL of BONES**. A skeleton makes a grab for Marvin the Mummy.

Who else is teetering on the plinths?

He looks hungry! Ha ha!

"**My bandages**!" he shrieks. "I'm unravelling!"
"Hang in there, Marvin," shouts Bird-Head Horace.
"I'll prise his **boney fingers** off with my crook."

But what's this?
SMASH! The bulldozers have started to demolish the
Museum. **CRASH**! Down comes a huge dinosaur's
Ribcage and traps the Ancient Egyptians.

Add a prehistoric ribcage crashing down on the Ancient Egyptians

"What a bunch of BONEHEADS!" ribs Captain Curse. "Now, we'll be 'avin' that Golden Howler Monkey, thankin' you kindly!"

The Museum is being smashed to its foundations!
The dinosaur's ribcage splits apart,
the walls are crumbling and plaster
is **falling** from the ceilings.

Finish the scene of ultimate destruction

Add a big bulldozer

Amazingly, everyone survives the demolition in one piece! Once the dust has settled, a tug of war begins.

"The Monkey is mine!" shouts Captain Curse.
"No, it's mine! Mine! Mine!" hollers King Crypt.
But the Golden Howler Monkey has **HAD ENOUGH**...

What lies buried beneath their feet?

A suit of armour

The Museum safe

"Stop it, all of you!" it shouts. "There's something you need to know."

An old motorbike

"I'm only made of **FAKE** gold, so stealing me won't make you rich," explains the Golden Howler Monkey. "But my singing is priceless! Let's start a band and become rich and famous rockstars!"

The Golden Howler Monkey is picturing his name in showbiz lights

Finish the chiming heads

Decorate the wall with popstars

Soon, they have a record deal. And a manager.
"Hey, guys," says Simon Towel. "I love your act.
I'm gonna make you **SUPER STARS!**"

Chapter 6
That's Showbiz!

The band is ready to go on tour! All aboard the
SPOOKY CREW mean machine!

Make the
tour bus
well cool

"Everyone on the bus go 'AHHHHHH'!" yells the Golden Howler Monkey. "Put the pedal to the metal!" And they're off!

When they arrive, some fans spot the Crew.
"Awesome!" they **SCREAM**, chasing the band down the street.

This fan is dressed like Marv

This fan has a crazed look in her eye

Draw an advert for something REALLY COOL here!

The Spooky Crew are a massive hit.
It's showtime! The **fans** go wild!

Add more
Spooky Crew
fans

"We really **LUCKED OUT** when we met the Golden Howler Monkey," laughs King Crypt, youthfully. "Now we have all the **IMMORTALITY OIL** we need!"

Finish the cheering Ancient Egyptians!

Who's celebrating here?

What a **spectacularly** spooky time they all had at the Haunted Museum! "We found the Golden Howler Monkey!" says Captain Curse.
"We met a sabre-toothed tiger," chuckles King Crypt.

"Then the Museum fell on our heads!" says Pharo-Nuff.
"But best of all," concludes the Golden Howler Monkey,
"we became mega-superstars!"

Picture Glossary

If you get stuck or need ideas, then use these pages for reference.

SEWER MONSTER

SKATEBOARDS

BOTTOM VIEW

TOP VIEW

If you like, you can copy the pictures. OR you can draw your own version.

SHOWING OFF

THE MUSEUM'S GUIDE

VEXED

HI THERE!

SHOCKED

Picture glossary

If you get stuck or need ideas, then use these pages for reference.

SAFE

A SKULL AFTER AN ARGUMENT WITH A PIRATE

MAMMOTHS

MAD

WITH VICTIM

Nikalas' MAMMOTH

WITHOUT VICTIM

Tim's MAMMOTH

HOPPING MAD

Visit our **awesome** website and get involved!

Website

MEGA MASH-UP

My Mash-up | Mega Draw | The Books | Ask Us | What's Next?

OUT NOW!

The first two books in the series

Breaking News!
This just in - a Haunted Museum is to be the scene of the next Mega Mash-Up! It's thought that some Pirates and some Ancient Egyptians will have a bit of a barney and CHAOS and MAYHEM will ensue! There'll be mummies

Click here to audition a character for our next book!

www.MEGAMASH-UP.COM
Upload artwork and get the latest news

Also available

MEGA MASH-UP
Aliens v MAD Scientists under the Ocean

MEGA MASH-UP
Romans v Dinosaurs on Mars

MEGA MASH-UP
Robots v Gorillas in the Desert